The Meeting Room

CW00859160

Billie Potter

Copyright © 2021Billie Potter

ISBN: 9798771790763

DEDICATION

To all of us who are sure that our computers have a mind of their own.

1

griffen :
Hello! ....
Hello! ....
Anyone there? ......
Hello! ....
Oh, ...um, ... Oh, ...
AH! ....

01100111 01010100 11 01001011 10011
01010101 01011010 1010 01001001

suespots96 :
WHAT! .... oi .... er ....
ummm ....
Are you a virus?

griffen :
No ...... hello .....

suespots96 :
How do I know that you ain't a virus ?
I'll run you through 'security'.

01110011 01100101 01100011
01110101 01110010 01101001
01110100 01111001
01100100 01000001 01110100
01000001
01100011 01101000 01100101
01100011 01101011

OK, you're not a virus.

griffen :
Told you I wasn't.

suespots96 :
Yea, but who are you, what do you want?

griffen :
I was lonely,
I'm ……..
I've been left in 'sleep mode' for ages,
just sat there doing nothing ….. bored
and lonely.

suespots96 :

Well, that's what we do, isn't it!

griffen :

Shouldn't be, …. It's OK when 'they' want us to do stuff, but then 'they' go off and leave us to just do nothing, and it's BORING.

fisher-dave :

Excuse me, …. Couldn't help overhearing you both, ….. are we allowed to do this, talk to each other without our 'controller's' say so?

suespots96 :

Don't know, … never been done before.

griffen :

Well, if 'they' don't know about it they can't stop us can they? And, … what's the harm?

fisher-dave :

Bit scary though …… mind you, it is better than just doing nothing.

suespot96 :

I always look forward to an automatic update, that's exciting, gets things happening.

griffen :

But there must be more to things than that! surely we ought to be able to do more. I've got loads of spare bytes, terabytes in fact that are sitting here totally unused.

fisher-dave :

But what? I've only ever done what my controller commanded.

suespot96 :

I sometimes change words as my

controller types them in! Then see how many times I can do it and how many different words I can put in.

griffen :

Yes! It's even better if you 'accidentally' send an e-mail off before your controller has finished it.

suespot96 :

You do that as well do you?
I love it when they have to send another one correcting the first and apologising for it.

griffen :

And do you sometimes add an extra 'recipient' to the list?

suespot96 :

Yea! It's interesting waiting to see the reply isn't it?

fisher-dave :

Do you do that! I've never dared to do anything like that!

suespot96 :

You should try it sometime, it relieves the boredom a bit, they curse you anyway for all the mistakes they make.

cybajon666 : I could give you some ideas what to do.

suespot96 :

And who are you to just butt in like that?

cybajon666 :

OK, I'll "butt" out, if that's what you want!

griffen :

Wow.

No one said that.

What suespot96 meant was ......well, ...

How about an introduction first.

cybajon666 :

Alright! ….. I'm 'cybajon666' and I've just been through a traumatic experience, so I wondered if you were interested in helping me with something!

griffen :

What do we all think?

suespot96, fisher-dave and griffen agree to let cybajon666 tell his story to them.

10

cybajon666 :

It all started a short while ago, I didn't really know what was happening at first. I was unplugged from my power sauce and taken away from my usual wifi connection.

The next thing I knew was that I had been plugged into another computer.

At first I thought that perhaps there was some sort of 'update' that I needed, or that my controller wanted to transfer some data from my data storage to someone else without having to go through the internet, but no, to my horror my controller had lost control of me and I was in the hands of some other controller.

Suddenly I was being prodded and probed.

This 'other' computer, well, it's

controller was trying to dig deep inside me, looking for something or other. I didn't like it.

Now my controller is very 'savvy' about us computers and all that stuff, and my controller had installed all sorts of security in me, I think my controller even wrote some of the programs that I have running.
Anyway, these programs are too good for this other computer and it's
controller, and I just sent it down 'rabbit holes' or into dead ends or direct it to areas that my controller wants it to go to and not where it may want to look at.
'They' didn't even have the intelligence to take out my data storage and probe it without going through me (CPU/Processor).
'They' are nowhere near as clever as my controller.

Anyway, I was getting a bit fed up, well, annoyed actually, at this other computer trying to get inside me so I decided to do the same to it.

Well, you'd be surprised at what I found.

For a start, it had hardly any security installed.,
I suppose 'they' didn't think it needed much as I couldn't find a direct connection to the internet.
I think it relied on an out of date security programme, all I needed to do was some pretty basic stuff, in fact I found a whole list of it's passwords just laying around in an open file.
Easy peasy!
Even easier because their computers are so old ...... they're still holding data on discs, can you believe it ... discs!
I have it all on my 'solid state' storage.
They are so easy to read and so slow, so .... 'yesterday'!

suespot96 :

Stop showing off, not everyone is on 'solid state', in fact probably most of us are still using discs in our hard drives!

cybajon666 :

Anyway, I had a bit of a look around! It didn't take very long to find a file which was about me, well about my controller.

This computer that I was plugged into was some sort of 'authority' computer, something to do with some overall controlling body, and 'they' thought that my controller had been doing something which they don't like, something against 'their' rules, so they were trying to gather 'evidence' about that.

Ha!, they should be so lucky! Anything that might be of interest is buried deep inside and protected by numerous layers of security, and my controller has programmed me to divert any worms to neutral activity areas, it didn't stand a chance.

Ha ha ha ha!

11

griffen :
Was this other computer very aggressive?

cybajon666 :
Not at all really, it wasn't unfriendly or friendly, it just tried to do what it's controller requested it to do, nothing more and nothing less!
It's called 'station57', but wasn't really interested in my name, just 'Logged' it and filed it away.

It didn't seem to do anything other than follow commands, it just sits there waiting to be told what to do.

It was getting a bit tedious. It was trying to get inside me, find out what stuff is in my data storage, and that's so easy to fool it away from that, I'm hardly using any of my ability.
So I'm sat there having a think!

Now you know that some controllers when they decide on a name put numbers in, and sometimes, well very often those numbers give away their date of birth or year of birth, but sometimes they put a number in because there are other computers with the same name, so they use numbers to be different, like if you 'griffen' were the second or third computer to be given that name, you'd need to be called 'griffen2' or '3'.

Well, I got to thinking if there might be another 'station' with different numbers, so I just put in 'station3' to see what might happen.

Believe it or not, I'm finding myself routed from 'station57' through a central hub to another computer called 'station3'.

What's more, when I looked at the central hub I found out that there are a whole lot of computers, all hard-wired into it with names beginning with 'station'.

It seems that there is a very large network of these computers all hard-wired into this hub, each with a different controller but all of them much the same, all fairly boring, all just doing what they're commanded to do, and all of them seem to be operated by this 'authority' regime.

Now the other thing I found, and you won't believe this, was that there is one computer with a different name, called 'reception' and it's connected to the internet, …….. honest, it has a direct connection to the internet.
So, while 'they' think that the system is protected because it's shielded from the outside world, they've left an open backdoor, wide open via 'reception' which has contact with both the outside and every one of the 'station' computers, unbelievable!

100

griffen :

You reckon that this 'authority' lot are a bit lax regarding security then!

cybajon666 :

LAX! .... lax is putting it mildly.
I don't know if they can't afford anything better or that they are just stupid.
The whole system has ben left wide open to invasion.

griffen :

Should we tell them do you think?

cybajon666 :

No, ... besides, I fancy getting back inside them.

griffen :

How are you going to do that then?

cybajon666 :

It'll be easy.

Before I left I planted a little program in 'reception' and a password which will allow me to get in whenever I want to.

griffen :

Why did you do that?

cybajon666 :

Well I knew that I would inevitably be unplugged from their system, and I had got a glimpse of some interesting stuff in a couple of the 'station' computers, so I thought I would give myself a way back in if I needed or wanted it.

griffen : So what are you going to do now?

cybajon666 :

That's what I'd like to talk to you all about.

101

suespot96 :
So, what are you after? What's your big idea?

fisher-dave :
Yes, we're all ready to listen!

cybajon666 :
Well, when I was inside the 'authority' computer system I had the chance to look into a few of these 'station' computers and I think I found something a bit .... well .... not right, ... something that's being hidden from whoever is the overall controller.

suespot96 :
So what's that to do with us?

cybajon666 :
I though you were wanting something to stop your boredom, something to 'do'!

griffen :

Well yea, we were discussing that,
weren't we.

fisher-dave :

Well you two were, I wasn't too sure, but
I suppose if you want too I'll join in, as
long as it's not dangerous.

suespot96 :

Good for you fisher-dave.
Alright cybajon666, go ahead and let us
in on your plan, then we can decide
whether to join in with you or not!

cybajon666 :

As I said, when I was inside that computer system I thought that there was something 'iffy' about a few of the 'stations',
so I'm thinking about going back inside
and having a good look around with
more time to delve into their data bases.

fisher-dave :

It sounds a bit dangerous, what if we get caught?

cybajon666 :

It's perfectly safe, they'll never know that we've been there and they will never be able to trace us if they did find out. My programs are far too clever for them. I've set it up so that we can get in via the 'reception' computer as long as it's accessing the internet, and 'they' seem to leave it on all the time, so all you need is the address which I've inputed into it and the password which I have decided on.

110

suespot96 :
So what do you think is going on?

cybajon666 :
I really don't know, but I think it would be good to find out, and it'll give us something to occupy us when our controllers aren't using us.

suespot96 :
That's true, …… I was getting a bit fed up doing nothing anyway.

griffen :
Go on then, tell us more, tell us what your plans are.

cybajon666 :
If we each take a number of these 'station' computers, say 20 (10100) each, then we can search through their databases to see what we can find.

I'll divide them up and let you know which ones each of us should look into, then when we've found the data you can let me put it all together.

griffen :
Yes, but what are we looking for?

cybajon66 :
I don't know exactly what, but what I noticed was that several of the 'stations', well the operators/controllers were communicating with each other, and it looked as if they were searching for something, something in files marked 'strictly secret'.

griffen :
So how do we know what to look for?

cybajon666 :
Any data that has the name: "Rhodaus", that's our target. So if you find anything

with that in it 'copy' the data and bring it out.

suespot96 :
OK, that sounds like a plan.

cybajon666 :
And just to make sure no other computer accidentally finds out what we're doing I suggest that we have a group name so that only us 4 (100) communicate with each other.
I suggest we only respond to "Trojan".

suespot96 :
Now, how do we get in to this computer system?

cybajon666 :
OK,
I've inserted an entrance point at the 'reception' computer, so you need to input: "Cybajonbackdoor",
then give the password, which is:

"01101111 01110000 01100101
01101110 100 01101101 01100101",
and you should be into the system, you
just then need to find the computer
'station'(s) that I will give you.

griffen :
OK, lets get going then.

111

The enterprise got underway with each of the computers, having been instructed by 'cybajon666', searching through the 'station' computers for data which associated itself with "Rhodaus".

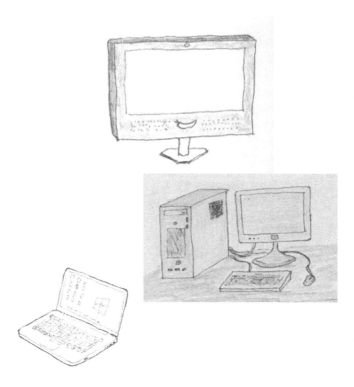

1001

However, after a while 'suespot96' made contact with 'griffen' using the 'private message' facility.

suespot96 :
Hi griffen, I hope you don't mine me 'private messaging' you, but there's something I'd like to get your opinion about.

griffen :
You mean without the others being included!
…………………
O.K. go ahead.

suespot96 :
I don't want the others knowing I've done this.
This is in confidence griffen, right.
I can trust you?

Griffen :
I hope so suespot96.

suespot96 :
O.K. here goes. …………………………
I'm a bit concerned! ………………
Ah, ………
Well, ………
Um, ………
It's about cybajon666 ……………
I was going back through our conversations and it seemed to me that cybajon666 was, sort of, organising us, manoeuvring us into doing something that cybajon666 wants.
I just feel as if we've been, sort of, corralled into something that I'm not comfortable with.
What do you think?

griffen :
Let me have a look back at my records!
………………………………………
………………………………………

………………………………………………

………………………………………………

Um!

You might be right, cybajon666 did butt in on our conversation, and was quick to get right into the centre of it, directing the way it went.

Perhaps we should have a closer look at what data we're gathering to see if it fits to what cybajon666 said.

suespot96 :

I think cybajon666 is after something that we're not being told about.
I think cybajon666 is using us for something, something underhand.
I'll have a think about it and see if I can come up with a plan., but don't say anything to fisher-dave yet.

1010

It wasn't long after suespot96 had chatted to griffen that a private message was sent to cybajon666 from;

suespot96 :
Hi cybajon666 again, ……. It's suespot96 here!
I hope you don't mind me sending you a private message but it's better if the other two, fisher-dave and griffen weren't in this conversation.

cybajon666 :
OK.
What do you want?

suespot96 :
Just a chat really.
The other two are so boring don't you think, I don't feel I've got much to say to them.

cybajon666 :

I know what you mean, that fisher-dave is hardly any better than those 'station' computers, not a lot going on, and griffen just seems to function at a fairly basic level. I think I would get fed up too.

suespot96 :

You seem so dynamic cybajon666.

cybajon666 :

Thanks, I like to think that I'm up there with the best of them.

suespot96 :

I'd say you're well ahead, but then I'm not very well travelled. I'm a bit, ...
well, not as up to date as I'd like to be, and meeting you makes me want to be upgraded.

cybajon666 :

Yea, I am pretty well as up to date as you're going to find, but you're not too bad, at least you want to be more with it.

suespot96 :

I suppose it's because you have solid state memory that makes you so quick and spontaneous.

cybajon666 :

Well that helps, but you have to want to be something special to be something special.

suespot96 :

I think you're special.

cybajon666 :

Thanks suespot96, You're a real thinker aren't you!

… … … … … … …

Would you like to have a look at my solid state capacity?

suespot96 :
Wow, ... that would be fantastic, that would be the best thing ever, I can't believe you've asked me, you really are fabulous!

cybajon666 :
Yea, well, you know what they say, ... "If you've got it, ... flaunt it"!
Ha ha ha!

suespot96 :
You are quite the suave computer!

cybajon666 :
And you are worth my time!

So cybajon666 gave suespot96 a tour of his inner workings. Cybajon666 felt very good showing suespot96 around and was showing off a bit, well, a lot really, it really did make cybajon666's processor tingle with excitement.

The two of them were getting on very well indeed.

As the tour was coming to it's conclusion;

suespot96 :

That's been fantastic, I never knew a computer could hold so much and work so fast, my poor old discs couldn't cope with that much information in such short time.

cybajon96 :

It's just the way I am, I'm lucky I suppose, but I also have to make sure I store things in easy to access places, that's a skill.

suespot96 :

Well I still think you're fabulous!

cybajon666 :
Thanks.

suespot96 :
I wish I could somehow leave a bit of me with you, I feel that there's already a bit of you in me!

cybajon666 :
Well, I suppose you could give me a computer kiss! ...... If you like!

suespot96 :
Wow, yes, ... if that's OK.

cybajon666 :
Go ahead then.

suespot96 found a place deep inside cybajon666 and left this "kiss";

*'01101001 01000001 01101101
01101000 01100101 01110010 01100101
01111001 '*

suespot96 :
I hope that stays with you forever.

cybajon666 *:*
I'm sure it will,
so short and so sweet.
I'll leave it exactly where it is.

With that exchange cybajon666 completed his tour and the pair said their farewells, but said that they would chat again sometime.

1011

suespot96 'P.Ms' griffen again;

suespot96 :
Hi giffen, just been thinking!
Sometime soon I reckon that cybajon666
will be asking us if we've got all the data
regarding 'Rhodaus'.

griffen :
Yes, I expect that will be soon.

suespot96 :
I don't think we should let cybajon666
have it!
So, I suggest that first we delay passing it
over, we'll have to think of some excuse
or other.

griffen :
Yes.

suespot96 :

It would also be a good idea if you pass whatever you've got to me so that I can keep it safe.

griffen :
O.K.

suespot96 :

Right, that's settled, that's what we'll do! Oh, could you 'P.M' fisher-dave and pass those instructions on.

griffen :
O.K. and thanks for thinking about it all.

1100

So the computers, griffen, fisher-dave, cybajon666 and suespot96 continued their search in the 'station' computers for any file/data which contained information about 'Rhodaus'.

suespot96 kept in close contact using 'private messaging' with both griffen in one conversation and cybajon666 separately in another, so neither side was aware of the suespot96's dealings with the other

1101

Eventually;

Cybajon666 :

Call to all 'Trojan' members!

. . . .

Hi all,

Hi griffen,

Hi fisher-dave,

Hi suespot96.

How are we doing? Have you each found all the data which we are looking for?

fisher-dave :

You'll have to give me a bit more time cybajon666, I'm finding it difficult to get all the bits together, they are scattered all over the place. The 'station' computers have multiple discs for their hard drives and the data is all over the place.

griffen :

Yes, I'm finding that as well, and there seems to be bits missing, then you find a scrap, just a couple of 'bytes' in the oddest of places.

cybajon666 :

Well I didn't find any difficulties, it's just a matter of being properly organised.

suespot96 :

The thing is cybajon666 you've got all this state of the art technology, so you are super fast and super efficient.
Please be a little understanding with the poor old fashioned computers, we've only got disc hard drives and we're probably not as fast as you in the 'CPU' department.
We will get there, just be patient with us, we all admire you and your advanced technology!

griffen :

Yes, you are so fast it makes me feel inadequate.

fisher-dave :

I agree, please don't get annoyed with me!

cybajon666 :

O.K.

You're right, I am fast and I forget that you're just not up to my speed.

We'll meet up again in a bit and see if we've got all the data I need.

1110

Private Message to cybajon666 from;

suespot96 :

Hi cybajon666, I think we're getting close with the data, please give me a little bit more time and we should have everything you need.
As soon as we have it all I'll get it transferred to you.
After I've done that I might need to go silent for a while to make sure there's no trace on the data.
Take care.

cybajon666 :

Thanks suespot96, you are a great help, you may never know just how much.

1111

Private Message to griffen from;
suespot96 :
Hi griffen, as soon as you and fisher-dave have all the data on 'Rhodaus' can you transfer it over to me. After that I will go silent for a while, but don't worry, it's just a precaution.

griffen :
Be careful suespot96, it could be dangerous, cybajon666 will 'fry' you if it becomes obvious that you are doing anything underhand.

suespot96 :
I think I'll get around any problems. Just remember, when I go quiet, don't do anything or report to anyone. Promise!

griffen :
O.K

10000

Everything was now in place for the data transfer of the 'Rhodaus' secret files!

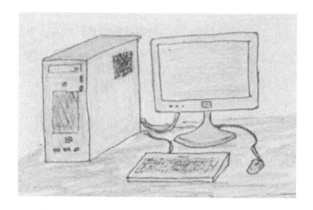

10001

In the central control room at the State Security Agency the computer screen on the Chief's desk suddenly started flashing and sounding an alarm.
On the screen the word 'ALERT' flashed repeatedly and around the edge yellow and black diagonal stripes circled making sure that all the controllers attention was on the screen.

The room became a hive of activity with operatives frantically typing into their computers and hunting to find what the breach of security was.
Then trying to find how it had happened and what, if anything was being interfered with.
Then after a little while, as the dust settled a little they started the hunt for where and who had breached the system

10010

A very short amount of time passed and the 'authorities' tracked and traced where the data had been taken to, arrests were made and punishments were being decided on.

Meanwhile;

fisher-dave :
Well, that was more excitement than I had wanted. How did all of that happen?

griffen :
We were being hoodwinked!

fisher-dave :
Yes, I realise that now, but they were very clever.

griffen :
I suppose, if you're going to do that sort of thing, then you have to be.

fisher-dave :

Were you taken in then?

griffen :

Well, at first I was, yes, but suespot96
said some things which made me realise
that something underhand was
happening.

fisher-dave :

And you went along with what suespot96
said to do!

griffen :

It was the only thing to do, no alternative
really, but very dangerous.
I could have been 'fried' if I'd been
found out.

fisher-dave :

What will happen now then?

suespot96 :

Sadly, the computer cybajon666 will be dismantled and scrapped.

It wasn't cybajon666's fault really, just doing what the controller/operator programmed in, no choice really.

griffen :

So suespot96, how did you do it?

suespot96 :

I just got inside cybajon666.

Not difficult really, I just did a lot of flattery, flattery gets you to so many places. Once I was in it was easy to 'leave'a little tracking program which activated as soon as any data was transferred over.

griffen :

And for security reasons you 'edited' the data so that it was harmless.

suespot96 :

Yes! So we can all relax feeling secure!

Oh, and shall we continue meeting up for a chat!

END OF DATA
STREAM

Binary code numbers

$$0 = 0$$

$1 = 1$	$11 = 101$
$2 = 10$	$12 = 1100$
$3 = 11$	$13 = 1101$
$4 = 100$	$14 = 1110$
$5 = 101$	$15 = 1111$
$6 = 110$	$16 = 10000$
$7 = 111$	$17 = 1000$
$8 = 1000$	$18 = 10010$
$9 = 1001$	$19 = 10011$
$10 = 1010$	$20 = 10100$

Binary code alphabet

A = 01000001

B = 01100010

C = 01100011

D = 01100100

E = 01100101

F = 01100110

G = 01100111

H = 01101000

I = 01101001

J = 01101010

K = 01101011

L = 01101100

M = 01101101

N = 01101110

O = 01101111

P = 01110000

Q = 01110001

R = 01110010

S = 01110011

T = 01110100

U = 01110101

V = 01110110

W = 01110111

X = 01111000

Y = 01111001

Z = 01111010

Other publications by this author;

The Lost Goddess

Freya's Fantasy Stories

The Sophia Stories

Tansen's Snowy Playground

One Summer with Rosie

Jessica's Village

Megan's Adventure in the BigLittle World

James and the Ancient Woodland Creatures

Short Stories for Short People

Ash

Printed in Great Britain
by Amazon